THE MIDNIGHT GAMES

THE MIDNIGHT GAMES

SIX STORIES ABOUT GAMES YOU PLAY ONCE

RHIANNON RASMUSSEN   M.B. HARE   CASEY LUCAS

M. LYN HALL   SHI BRIGGS   VELES SVITLYCHNY

ILLUSTRATED BY
ANDREY GARIN

Robot Dinosaur Press
robotdinosaurpress.com
PRINT ISBN 978-1-0879-8604-3
EBOOK ISBN 978-1-0879-8606-7

for the gamers

don't get played

CONTENTS

THE BURNER GAME_
RHIANNON RASMUSSEN

YOU PLAY THE GAME LIKE THIS. YOU GET TEN
of your friends together in the same room.
You each have a burner cell phone. You and
your friends hold the phones up to your
head. You all hit call at the same time, each
phone directed to the number to the friend
sitting to your left. You let the phones ring
to voicemail until the last click, when one
phone connects and someone—*something*
—impossible answers.

You may ask it questions, so long as you
are ready to hear the answers. And it will
take as many answers from you as you
request from it. Answers you may not want
your friends to hear. It knows when you lie.

Of course it's dangerous. That's half the
thrill, isn't it?

You read these instructions for the fifteenth time and think, who the hell has ten friends in the same city these days? Let alone with the same day off. Burner phones, though? That's easy. You get ten knockoff flip phones for cheap online. Bundle deal.

On friends, you end up compromising. You've never been popular, and that didn't change when you moved away from home, but you've always been a problem-solver. You rig up a simple little system to have the burners call each other at the exact same time, down to the tenth of a second, on speaker so that you can answer the last phone. The one that makes it through. The one that reaches the monster.

If any of them do.

You had ten friends back in high school. Sitting on the dirty floor of your basement, corners still damp from the receding winter, you'd played this game. That time no one had answered. Your aftermarket phones your so-called friend swiped from the back room of a repair shop all went to voicemail like they were supposed to. No unearthly voice answered the ouroboros call. You were disappointed, then. You decided it was because none of them had any questions worth answering. You didn't even throw out the phones after, like you were supposed to. Why throw out something you could make a buck on? Not a dollar from need, but a dollar from want, possibility stretching out before you, childlike.

You were all just kids. You didn't know desperation. You handed the silver-plastic phone back and wondered what a kid like you could possibly need to know so badly that it would bend reality?

Too bad you found out, a few weeks after graduation. Unfair, wasn't it? Just like that, possibility shortened to the other side of a door you couldn't open. So you just picked up and moved, trying to get away from the door, from the pity in your former friends' eyes, the apologies, the asides that were supposed to be supportive. You thought that would be better. That new people and new experiences would make the pain fade faster.

But it didn't. Pain had made a home in you. You couldn't move far enough away to lose it. You only wanted to know how long you had to wait before you could breathe again. Before you could live again, without this glass bomb ready to shatter inside of you at any moment.

So now, sitting on the thin rug covering the linoleum floor of your barren studio apartment, you set your ten cheap phones to dial, and you call.

The burners ring. Once. Twice. Three times. It's been a long time since flip phones. You see the ghost of your reflection in their glass. Each phone asks if you want to interrupt your call to take the incoming call, dim screens blinking red, surrounded by your own electronic summoning circle. They're the only lights in the room. The ringing is so regular that you could breathe to it, if your breath wasn't knotted in your chest.

Then they go to voicemail.

All except one. One where the screen goes blank with the click of a lock in a door.

You wait. It's not the breath you can't release in your chest that hurts so badly. It's the pain you can't escape, the one that moves with you.

The silence on the line sounds like a flourescent light going bad. There's breathing, or static. You wait, just to be sure, you tell yourself, but the call doesn't disconnect. Not even after the other phones close their voicemails, one-tenth of a second after each other.

"Hello?" you ask, and you hate how tinny your voice sounds. A bad connection, or no connection at all. Your sink, half-empty closet, your unswept cold floor, none of it bolsters your voice. "Hello?"

"You again," the monster says. You're not sure what you expected the voice of a monster to sound like, but it wasn't like this. The voice on the end of the line sounds... reasonable. A bit amused, even. Dry. Like someone trustworthy. Someone who will tell you the truth.

"Who are you?" you ask, before you remember the rules of the game.

"Your first question," the monster says, and you swear the static on the line takes the shape of a crooked little smile. "I am the one you were trying to reach. Often I say those who call me may have as many answers as they will give to me, but how *unusual* for you to call alone. A clever trick. I'll allow it—once. Let's be traditional. You may have three."

A silence. You open your mouth to

speak your next question, but the monster cuts you off with a crackling bark of a laugh.

"My turn. Where did all your friends go?"

Three, and you wasted one. Two was enough, wasn't it? And this one was easy. Basically a gimme. "I left them behind when I moved. I'm tired of everyone looking at me with pity in their eyes, saying *oh, you're so young to be dealing with something like this.* I wanted to meet new people who don't know, who don't compare me to how I was before."

The monster chuckled. "But you haven't met them. Your next question."

The pain your chest grows, down to the numb tips of your fingers. How do you even say this? "When does it stop?" you ask, and your voice catches. But the monster already knows. Even cashiers at the checkout know in the minute you interact with them. Even strangers stop just short of asking you what's wrong. The pain is in your shoulders, your spine, the dark pockets under your eyes. "When do I get to be whole again?"

"You don't," the monster says, so easily.

So casually. "Other people, maybe. But not you." And the pain and the anger at how easily those goring words come to it breaks more out of your chest; not a question, but a cry.

"Why me?"

"Because you are a coward."

"Even for the most shining examples of humanity, of which you are not, wounds do not vanish. You have scars and bruises and once breached the wound opens more easily the second time. But for you, especially you, it is because you ran. You saw her struggle, her love, her need for you and you closed the door on her and you left. Surely there are more important things to do than watch someone die, you thought. Surely its worse to die and see me dying alongside you looking at you looking at you as though you are a stranger, a broken bird, spiritless, a bought plot and granite waiting for a swiftly approaching date to be engraved on it. You thought, I will simply leave and the pain will leave with me and that will absolve me of not being able to walk you to the grave.

"She said she understood. That she knows you love her whether or not there is an absence at her side. But tell me, Did you run from love, because you could not bear to see the loved one wither, or from fear, because you knew when she looked at you, searching for support, she would see disgust?"

You cannot answer, because your mouth is dry.

"Whatever admirable quality it is that allows people to care for each other—you simply don't have it. So she died in the company of strangers who gave her more care than you could muster. Many people can look death in the eyes with compassion, but not you. And you will fear it and run from it at any chance you get. You will not have partners nor children, because when you look at them, hale, resting, waking, sleeping, you only see the chance for sickness in them. You grieve not that people die, but that they can die at all, and a thing that can die is the same as one that is dead.

"And tell me, can you ever love a dead thing, truly?"

"No," you whisper, and you and I both know that the monster tells the truth. ◆

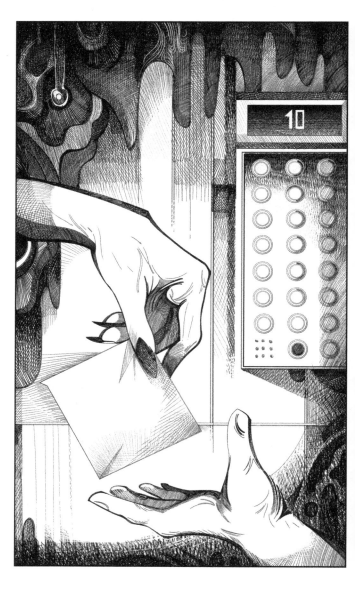

THE ELEVATOR GAME_
M.B. HARE

THERE ARE WAYS TO MEET THE LONG WOMEN,
if you wish.

*Firstly, find a building with ten floors or
more. Go alone, because we are terribly shy
and will flee from embarrassment if anyone
else enters your game—our game. There
should be a set of beautiful buttons before you.
I want you to touch them. I want you to feel
their bright clean plastic. I want you to press
four and two and seven and two and ten and,
finally, five.*

*Please stay in the elevator. Don't get out, or
we won't be able to meet.*

*At the fifth floor, I will arrive—or perhaps
one of my lazy sisters. You'll know me by my
beauty, but I won't mind if you talk to the
others. I'll forgive you.*

There are other steps you can find that come after this, but they don't lead anywhere interesting. Besides, I'd like to talk to you.

I think that you're extraordinary. I would love to talk to you. I'll listen to everything you say.

I think I like you, little one.

————

THE OTHER LONG women must learn to pace themselves. The blood will not stop flowing in the wound of the world. Not today and not tomorrow. We have done our jobs. We replenish. Things are going to be okay.

My claws dig into the flesh of the nearest cruciform—the red crosses that fill the shivering sky of our home, the living wound that made us and asks for nothing in return but company and sustenance. Long women sink their claws into the cruciform and burrow their mouths into Her, guzzling and gossiping, barking jokes or whispering kisses into devil-pointed ears. We can hear the little drops of blood onto the false concrete. For a while, when I was new, I timed my sips to make music.

Everything is false here, but comfortably so. We live in a Disneylanded place, an entertaining echo of the human world dreamt into being by our cruciform mothers. Mostly our worlds are empty, which is fine by me. You can't properly appreciate an imitation when it's crowded and loud. Some of my memories are from a girl who loved amusement parks, so I think about that sort of thing a lot.

I dig my hindclaws deeper into the mother wound and stretch my arms out. My arm-joints shatter comfortably. For a lovely second my spine tears and I dangle humorously from the cruciform. My eyes jiggle inside and look over the empty shadow of a town, some nowhere in Ohio.

I prefer hunting grounds like that. Famous landmarks are distracting, and the Long women who frequent them are very pretentious. The Otherworld New Yorkers write menacing slam poetry.

Can you believe that? Come on, now.

A few nearby Long women open their pores to speak bone music, a practice stolen from the Night Gaunts. It's embarrassing. My nervous system regenerates; I crawl down the wound to hang near the dirt and pretend that oh, them? I don't know them.

We're all antsy, when you get right down to it. it's getting late and we're all waiting for that damn bell to ring. The elevators have been running slow recently. It happens, though, and we'd still be complaining if they were running too fast. (Can you imagine how boring life would be if there was nothing to complain about?)

And, all savior-like in our moment of need, lo and behold: the bells ring out to us...

...or rather, the bells ring out to *me*. Marvelous luck of mine, that the other Longs are too absorbed in their feedings and whisperings to notice. Well, if they'd rather bicker and gossip than serve our mothers, that's their business. Ungrateful louts.

I memorize the tiny vibrations of the ringing bell, hold the space and place of them in my imagination long after the sound has echoed. I scutter across imitation walls; they have the texture of plaster but cling my claws like meat. I get into character, think about the sort of person our visitor must be: bored or curious or hungry for attention. I ask a window for permission and she allows me to slip through without cracking the glass. I scramble across the tiled hallway,

and I reach the elevator.

Its two metal teeth clamp shut. Behind the doors stands our little visitor, hypnotized by their own ritual in the corner, waiting for us to give them life.

My fingers are long and many-jointed. This helps when one must pull one's bones into a human shape. And mold the flesh. And scoop the accumulated fluids to be reabsorbed in hidden pouches, for cruciform mother despises waste. Sometimes the arrival hears the noises we make, sometimes they don't. Both possibilities entertain me.

The elevator senses that I'm finished and opens with a little *ting!* There stands our interloper in the corner, facing away like a good girl, a reasonable girl, does.

There's a joke to the ritual, and it goes like this: the performer is not supposed to look at us, to talk to us. Do you understand the joke yet? If not, take a moment.

Here it is: the only people in your world who would be dare to perform this ritual, who would think it was at all worthwhile, would dash themselves against the rocks of another world...that sort of person *will* talk to us. *Always* talks to us. Why? Loneliness, I suspect. Curiosity, too. Some didn't expect anything to happen at all, and break the rules in a sort of idiotic ecstasy because they know that the world is bigger and darker than they could've imagined, and wish to know it utterly.

This is not a wish that we can grant, but we do have experiences to offer.

The prey of today waits in the elevator corner. She is tall and blonde and unwashed. College-age. Her dress is dirty, but its bright blue flower patterns are welcome. All color in this place curdles here into off-whites or reds, the color palette of a mouth. Blues are brief miracles. Blues are the best wrapping paper for meat.

What might she like to hear?

"It's okay," I tell her. "You don't have to say anything if you don't want to. I understand."

She shuffles in the corner—you see, she's created a problem for herself. She can't look at me, can't talk to me, but she needs to press the elevator buttons to continue our game.

And so I stand in front of them, and I smile. (My teeth are enticingly sharp. These sorts love sharp teeth.)

My prey turns. (If I were one of my sisters, I'd be drooling now, but I would never.) Her long blonde hair swings around, and...

Her eyes are closed. She is smiling back at me, and her eyes are closed.

The girl lurches forward, blindly fumbling for the buttons, and yes, I *do* step aside for her—I'll admit that—but only because I loathe being touched. She thwumps against the metal panel and punches the first floor with her fat fingers.

I should say something. I *have* to say something.

"You've really thought about this," I say at once. A mistake—you never compliment unless it gets your hooks in. "You must have so much time for these things," I add.

She faces me now—an unnecessary risk on her part, which infuriates me more —and she is *still smiling*, and do you know what she does?

She shakes her head. She doesn't say a word, but she shakes her head.

The elevator shakes. We're rising to the tenth floor, where the Otherworld opens, and it occurs to me that she may actually get there. This smug little shit, just *throbbing* with blood that I cannot touch, may actually step out of the elevator into the Otherworld.

Perhaps this calls for a different tact. "Why don't we put our cards on the table, little one? What do you want?"

She laughs at me hoarsely. This does not break the rules. I fantasize about breaking her neck.

"The instructions you're following are flawed, you know. You pushed the wrong button earlier...but I guess you don't care, do you?"

She nods. I look at her more closely now: she's computer-light pale, with sleepless olive circles around her eyes. She is practically vibrating with excitement.

"Well," I say, "I'm glad *you're* having fun."

She shrugs. I lean back into the opposite corner to her. The air fills with the wet slapping sounds of architectural tendons working to transport this still-living human meat into the Otherworld.

The whole thing is incredibly embarrassing.

"I hope you know that this part takes longer than you'd think." About ten minutes, in fact. "You're here with a being from another world. Isn't that interesting?"

Nod.

"Don't you have any questions?"

Nod.

"Alright, then," I say. "So..."

The elevator chugs along. I turn away from her and try to get my bearings—no one will ever let me live this down. The girls will talk. And the cruciforms are capable of mockery. In fact, they're better at it than you.

She taps me on the shoulder (I cannot *believe* that she taps me on the shoulder) and hands me a sheet of paper.

It says:

"Hello! My name is Hanna! I'm a bit of an urban explorer, and I decided to branch out a little bit. Please fill out the following survey, could you?"

What a joke. I snarl in her face.

She offers a pen.

Does she think she's toying with me? Is that it? I snatch the pen from her hand and consider snapping it between my fingers. But then again, getting to know your prey *is* valuable. The hunt is a delicate dance of feints and tricks and...ugh, *fine.*

Are you or were you ever a human being?

We are the Long Women. We hunger and mock.

"You can't even read these answers right now," I say. "I don't know what you're getting out of this."

She shrugs.

What is the Otherworld?

An extension of the Cruciform Mothers. It hungers. It latches. It dances in the nowhere places, where

Shit. The paper tears a little. I pressed too hard with the pen. "Sorry," I say automatically. "That, you know, your paper is so cheap. And your dress is tacky."

Why elevators?

It was stairways once, but that was before my time.

"I should tear this up right in front of you," I say. She nods.

Oh my god, this bitch.

Is there a God?

Do you think I know? Do you think I care?

"What are you, a priest?"

She laughs. Yeah, I didn't think so.

What's your favorite color?

I can't write blue. If I write blue, what if she thinks I'm talking about her dress? But red is the color of business. Red is food. It's not a *favorite*, it simply is.

My favorite color is turquoise.

"You're going to die very soon, you know."

She shakes her head.

"Such confidence."

The elevator reaches its destination. The doors open. The false cities beckon; the red crosses slash the sky. There is no escape here, not really. Crossing the threshold changes you, gives us a piece of you even if you make it home. We plant those pieces in the fertile concrete, and—

Well, I can't just tell *all* the secrets.

Would you like to do this again next week?

I look at the paper, then at her.

"Come on, now."

But she isn't leaving the elevator.

She's supposed to leave the damn elevator.

"People are going to talk," I say. She giggles. Poor choice of words on my part. "About your death, that is. You see, you die if you don't leave the elevator. The buttons, ah...they..."

I will never hear the end of this for the rest of my life. If she doesn't leave the elevator, I have to leave alone. If I leave alone, I don't get to eat.

Would you like to do this again next week?

I nearly slash the words into the paper —**I am going to slip the bones from your still-living flesh and suck the marrow as you watch**—hand it back, and step to the other side of the threshold.

At which point she opens her eyes.

They match her dress.

"See you then!" she says brightly, and the doors clang shut. ◆

THE SYNCHRONIZATION GAME_
CASEY LUCAS

I TAKE THE BEND IN THE PENINSULA HIGHWAY faster than I should. Now that you're not gripping at my shoulders, holding tight to my back, I have no reason to be cautious. I lean into the curve and try not to think about the things I want tonight, the things I want to witness. I let gravity tilt my body and my bike as it will, gripping with my thighs, and the horizon unspools all at once. Rain-slick pavement, bedraggled evening clouds, mile after mile of sea. Grey on grey on grey.

I'm rolling into the layby forty minutes late, but nobody says anything. They've already got the mirror set up, its glass obscured by the drape of a heavy curtain. I look past their faces, Alec and Mo and

Benji, and I feel like I've returned to the scene of a crime, a firestarter standing in the crowd, watching my friends hose down the wreckage.

They've assured me in the past they don't see it that way. That they're here because they want to help. That they help because they care.

The game goes like this: one mirror in the room. One mirror inside the camera. A heavy cloth and a lens cap to veil any and all reflections when the mirrors are not in use. Though the details differ from between telling, little tics of language and medium and character limits and slang, the mirrors never change.

Rituals like these, they're a fractal bloom across the internet, mirrors and linkbacks unfolding even as each tiny iteration transmutes them into something new. We'd taken ours from a comment someone left on Stack Overflow, because by instinct I trusted them more than Reddit. Mo said that was ridiculous—we're hunting ghosts, not looking for a regex cheat sheet and—

I'm stalling, aren't I.

I unpack my camera, shake out my

helmet hair, and walk over to the mirror to set up my tripod.

The guys did the best they could, angling the mirror toward the tightest part of the bend in the road. I'm not sure if it's my imagination, but if I squint, I think maybe I can still see the faintest streaks of black across the asphalt, remnants of two parallel tire treads, a skid of rubber across the road. This autumn has been a wet one, though. And it's been three months since the accident. Maybe I can't see anything at all.

Maybe there's no evidence left that you were ever here.

But tonight, if it's out there to be found, we might find evidence of the thing that killed you.

My camera's a big, bulky Canon, the heavy kind that feels good in the hands. I take my time adjusting the tripod and screwing a heavy hood onto the lens. None of the posts online say anything about whether rain on the lens will irreparably ruin your ritual, but I'm not leaving anything to chance.

When I'm finished, the camera faces the shrouded mirror. The mirror faces the chalky, sea-battered cliffs, angled so that it captures the snug curve of the road. The wind kicks up. I taste salt. It helps ground me, helps drag me out of the memory fog that threatens if I linger here too long.

"Hey." Mo's been snapping his fingers near my face. I'm not sure how long. "You sure you're cool?"

"Yeah," I promise, sounding far more confident than I am. "Always."

There's sea-spray on his lashes. I notice that when he bends in close, his dark eyes tight with concern.

"You don't have to do this," he said. "And you *definitely* don't have to do it alone. One of us could—"

I shake my head. He cuts himself off. All the things he says are true, the way that gravity exists and sugar is bad for me: a distant, objective truth that doesn't matter in any concrete ways. Nobody is making me do this. Nobody is holding a gun to my head. Nobody *makes* you have that second slice of cake at a birthday party. But Mo, for all he cares, he doesn't get it. Doesn't understand that wanting this is all I know now.

I grab Mo by the forearm and squeeze

his sleeve. "You guys have done enough. More than enough."

In the blurry immediate aftermath of the accident, Mo and the others had been more of a fixture in my house than I was. I don't even remember who called who, how they knew to show up, who suggested they do all that cooking and cleaning and grocery shopping and fishtank-cleaning. I watched them move through the space I used to share with you like they belonged there, like they were fighting harder to keep it livable than I was. I was a ghost by comparison, reduced to a haze that drifted through the halls, an indistinct haunting in my own home even though you were the one who died.

I look down. My boots have left little wet footprints on the roadside. Today I am real.

The game goes like this: the principal player waits for dark. Once night has fallen, they light a candle at the foot of the mirror. Then they wait. They wait however long it takes, until the moment the candle burns out. The moment the flame is snuffed, so the ritual says, the player can aim their camera at the mirror and pull the shutter. And if they're quick enough...

I release Mo's arm and look away.

They all assume it's you I'm hoping to see.

Benji pulls a pack of candles from his pocket. They're big, ugly, and yellow-green, the citronella kind that promise to repel mosquitos with a money-back guarantee. Whatever. They'll do. I give him a game smile and stoop to set the candle up.

"Last chance to back out," says Mo. "Hell, I could do it. I don't mind."

I want to thank him for giving me an out. For saying it all in that tone of voice that promises he knows I'm hard, knows I wouldn't bail from some lack of bravery. But bravery isn't the issue here. It is not an act of bravery to step out onto a bridge when an abyss is yawning up behind you.

"We won't be far," Mo promises. "Call us as soon as it's done. Whether it's..." He visibly stumbles over choosing a suitable word. "Whether it works or not."

I turn my head in the direction they go. I hear an engine. I am aware of the shape of a car, slick-gliding silver in the grey-on-grey landscape. All this happens but I don't really watch them go. It's like my eyes are already watching somewhere else.

The sky grows dark, and it isn't long before the sun dips behind the cliffs. There's something incongruous and backwards about living on the east coast - sunsets feel like they should take place over the sea. Here, the hills claim the sun and the water simply grows dark.

With wind-chilled fingers, I light the candle at my feet. I step behind the tripod and grip the corner of the drape that veils the mirror.

The road lays behind me, a serpent at my back. I am alone with the things I carry: my memories, my regrets, all the things I withhold, and you.

ALCOHOL MAY HAVE BEEN A FACTOR IN FATAL ROLL CRASH, SAY POLICE

Citronella and sea-smell. I breathe in hard and hope my fingers will be quick. I've chewed off all my lip balm but I'm too afraid to grab for more.

What if I miss the moment?

What if I screw it up?

What if I don't?

The game goes like this: if the player times their shot right, their camera will glimpse where their eyes cannot. A photo of the world beyond our own, taken at that liminal moment when darkness falls, when the gauzy border between real and unreal is at its thinnest.

I don't think you're out there, haunting the pavement. I'm not sure I even think ghosts are real.

But in the moments before impact—another liminal place and time, a borderland, the moment between action and reaction, between choice and consequence, between Before and After—you saw something.

You screamed that you saw something. And then you wrenched the wheel, determined to avoid it. Then we crossed into that borderland together.

The candle flickers at my feet.

My mind returns to the scene of the crime. The moment when I awakened, tangled in the umbilical of my seat belt, glass-glitter shards wreathing us like stars.

You gasped and gurgled, palms to the window, your mouth a river of red.

I tried to help, arms jellied with adrenaline, and I reached for your seat belt and couldn't feel it and couldn't find it and geometry got slippery and horror hiccuped my breath in my throat when I realized you must not have been wearing yours. Because that's the only way your front could be facing me when your legs were still—

The candle flickers at my feet. I am alone with the things I withhold.

I told the others you died on impact. I didn't want your mother to know you suffered. I didn't want the guys to know you cried.

Maybe the cops were right. Maybe *alcohol was a factor.*

Maybe your final words were just the last, confused synapses of a dying mind trying to make sense of what it perceived. What the remnants of its eyes could see, what its memory dredged up in its final battered moments.

When I tried to free us from the wreckage, you grabbed my wrist, blood-slick grip hard as iron.

Don't go out there, you whispered wetly, even as the car began to fill with smoke.

I saw it. It's out there.

It looked just like you.

The candle flickers and goes out. I pull the curtain and hit the shutter, trusting reflex and gravity. I smell burning. I need to know what you saw.

Somewhere, glass is cracking and shattering.

Somewhere, a car is streaking through the air.

Somewhere, the mirror in my camera is syncing with a mirror to somewhere else.

Somewhere, we are stepping into the borderland. ◆

THE DICE GAME_
M. LYN HALL

I'M STILL PLAYING. THE NOISES HAVE stopped, but it hasn't yet been twenty-four hours since we started.

"Can I get you some coffee?" I ask.

"What? Oh, yeah." Sam throws his coat over the arm of the couch.

The drapes do nothing to block out the morning light. It pounds at my skull, making my nose run and the skin of my face feel swollen. I'm sure Sam can see it, but he doesn't say anything yet. He will.

I can't see his face, only a limned silhouette. The shape is unfamiliar: he should have a beard, but the smooth plane of his jaw catches the light instead. I keep thinking the face inside that circle of shadows will be a stranger's when he steps into my dim kitchen.

It's still his face, though.

Sam casts a look down the dark hall to our bedroom. A strip of lamplight peeks out from under the door.

"Just wanted to check on you," he says, stepping around a couple of boxes. "How's packing? All those books must weigh a shitton."

"Makes you regret ever buying them." I laugh mechanically. "There's a box over there full of yours, by the way. I keep finding shit you forgot to take."

"Oh, no." Sam laughs. I fill the coffee maker and turn it on. The gurgling starts. My belly gnaws and twists, sick and hungry at the same time.

Sam's noticed the empty cat bowl. He starts clicking his teeth and making little kiss noises to nobody. "Must be hiding," he says.

"I don't know where she is," I lie. "I saw her just this morning." For now, it's silent beyond the bedroom door.

Sam looks over his shoulder down the hall before he sits in the kitchen chair. "She's probably sleeping. Anyway, uh..."

Here it is. I know his voice and his tone, even if he has a stranger's baby-face. "How are you doing? We haven't talked in a while. You said you'd call me last week."

"I'm okay. It's just hard."

There's a familiar look in his eyes, too: is it just the move? he wants to ask. *The eviction*, I would correct him. But that isn't the question underneath the question. I can feel him looking in the kitchen, as if every cabinet door could hide my dirty glasses and my bottles, my boxes, my stain. As if that's what I'm hiding this time.

———

I USED to love games like this as a teenager. I had a friend once—on a forum I've long since forgotten about—who claims they used to play the dice game once a week, wagering for things like gas money and free drinks. It became a part of their weekly landscape, a little magic just for them. You don't have to ask for a million dollars or a cure for cancer. You just have to *want* what you ask for, otherwise it's an insult to him.

I never thought to try until a few months ago, after Sam left me and took

Jason. Last night, a week after I lost my job, I did it. I wasn't expecting anything but figured it couldn't hurt to try.

This is how the game works, according to most accounts I found on the web. You need a gameboard, but the board can be from any game, and you need two six-sided dice. Those can also be from anywhere. Lastly, you need a cup you can't see through.

You'll never see who you're playing it with, so make sure you're alone in the room you've chosen. That the windows are blocked off.

The first time I played, I laid the checkers board across the coffee table with reverent attention. I used a paper cup. I had the curtains drawn tight.

After everything's laid out, you address him politely. State your wager, then roll. Drop the die into the cup on his side of the board, with the cup facing up. Leave the room for no less than seven and no more than eleven minutes. Come back in.

If the cup's face-down, he wants to play. If, when you uncover the die, his roll is lower than yours, you get what you asked for.

Last night, my first time, I asked for sobriety.

I left my Schrödinger's cup face-up with his die in it. I went to stand out on the landing, where the winter chill stung my cheeks. I set an alarm for seven minutes and waited one more for good measure. When I went back in, the cup was turned over, the die spilled out.

This is how you know you've pissed him off. Even if you did everything right. They say when this happens that you're supposed to take the board out of the room and burn it, along with the cup. You're supposed to dispose of the dice, too. You're never supposed to play the game again. Twenty-five hours ago, I thought about throwing it all away.

But I didn't get to play the game. I did everything right. It wasn't fair.

———

THE CHAIR CREAKS as Sam starts to look over his shoulder and down the hall again, then stops. I wonder what he thinks is in the bedroom.

"How's Jason?" I ask. Behind me, the coffee maker gargles.

"Oh, great." Sam smiles wire-taut. Familiar. "I just dropped him off at Mom's for the weekend."

"When can I see him?"

Sam looks at me, eyes hooded. His lips press together.

Not for the first time, I'm aware of hate crawling up my spine. The way he looks at me boils in my churning belly. I used to know him and him me, twined together at the roots. The start of a family. He grows up and up. I wither, untangled. He let me keep the cat, at least.

The floorboards creak. The first time, Sam notices, but it might've been the yawn of old wood. The second time, I see him start to look over his shoulder at the door to the hallway and then stop. We hear a rattle and a click.

"Is that Tufts?" Sam asks. "Maybe he's shut up in the bedroom." He starts to get up.

"Don't," I say.

———

THE BOARD RASPED and clattered as I laid it out on my bedding among the old wine stains. I was angry at him now. If he wanted me to respect him, he ought to have respected me. My bedroom wore its usual perfume of sweat and old sheets for the occasion.

I set the plastic cup on the other side of the board and dropped the die inside. I rolled my own without preamble. Five dots faced up. "I want to be happy again."

I couldn't hear anything but tinnitus and my own breathing. The light didn't change. A tawny, fluffy shape—Tufts—slunk across the floor, fur on end, to tuck itself into the shadows underneath the desk. Her eyes flashed there.

I poured more wine, twisting the neck so it didn't spill. A few droplets hit the board.

When I left and shut the door behind me, the hall was dark. A little light leaked out the kitchen door. I checked the time on my phone. One fifteen. I slumped back against the door, resting my head. Then I was sitting on the hardwood floor. Then I shut my eyes.

I opened them. The pain at the base of

my skull was sharper. My teeth tasted black. Nothing was different about the light, but when I took out my phone, it was two in the morning.

Forget the game. What was I doing?

I got up and took my glass to the kitchen. I dumped the dregs into the sink. A creak sighed from down the hall, accompanied by the clatter of a die. I dropped the glass in the sink. Watched it break. The floorboards squealed.

If you wait too long, the post says, you have to leave the door shut for twenty-four hours. *That's not too hard,* I thought, a nasty chill still threatening to climb out of my skin. I listened to the sounds of someone moving around in my bedroom.

I cleaned up the glass. Just twenty-four hours.

His steps were irregular, buoyant, skipping too far apart. If he was pacing, he sounded like a dancer. I stood silent for a long time at the sink, listening. Tap-tap, tap, tap-tap-tap. I heard something that sounded like an inhale, then a long exhale.

———

"PLEASE," I say.

"What the fuck is wrong?" Sam demands, like the first spurt of water through a crack in a dam. "What's in there? Is somebody in there?"

"You always used to do this! It's none of your business."

"You've been drinking, I can tell. Do you even want to see our son again?"

"I'll let Tufts out after you leave. I promise. It's just the cat."

"You obviously still need me," Sam mutters, standing up from his chair. The floorboards creak again. "I'll do it, then, if it's *just the cat*." He turns and starts down the hall.

"It's none of your—"

He disappears. The doorknob rattles. The door opens. I brace myself white-knuckled on the counter. The door slams shut and rattles in its frame.

A noise like the low baying of a dog in pain. Sam calls my name, then gargles into animal incomprehensibility. It doesn't last long. My clay-lump feet walk me to the hall. I freeze when I see the door, shut. More footfalls. A heavy rasp, like someone being dragged. Then, nothing.

I stand still.

I cross to the door. When I open it, Tufts spills out and jets down the hall behind me. The room is as I left it, empty and small with its one covered window, the lamp still on from last night.

The checkers board is still on the bed.

The cup is turned over. ◆

 THE HOSTING GAME_
SHI BRIGGS

MY WATCH TELLS ME IT'S 12:33 AM. WITH shaking hands, I fold the last napkin for the table setting, and laboriously lay it down on a mint colored dinner plate. One of four.

A table sits in what used to be my bedroom. In the center of the table squats a pedestal, a plant holder I've repurposed as the centerpiece. It bears the remnant of a once-large candle, and a single sheet of stationary, pen waiting on top. I ignore it, and rearrange the sorry assortment of offerings I've gathered.

There isn't much food left, not after all this time. Vienna sausages, slick with congealed fat, speared through with bamboo picks. Graham crackers coated in a greasy, gritty, buttery spread. Hard, dry, cracked cheese speared through with bamboo picks. Too-soft olives in threes, speared through with bamboo picks. Globby punch. A dearth of plenty. I check my watch, as if it matters. 1:46 am.

I gather my box of matches and shake it, but I've counted. I know there's only four. They rattle around desperately inside of the box. Just enough. I light one, and use it to light the candle on the pedestal. My lips tighten against my teeth as I back away, letting the match burn until it hits my fingers and I have to drop it. I grind it into the bare hardwood floor. I turn to stalk the length of my house.

Every window is covered, various textiles nailed into place like skins stretched out to dry on racks. Throws, the summer blankets, the winter blankets— when I ran out, towels, shower curtain, rugs, my favorite dress, stretched tight to black out all the natural daylight I'd paid the extra for. Every room now tinted only with off-white bulbs. My electricity had never gone out. A small comfort, and one I'd be leaving behind.

I reach the entryway, and brush off the front of my second-favorite dress, clutching the box of matches to my chest, checking my watch. Still 1:46 am.

I take in a breath, my dry lips stick together, slowly peeling open. "I'll be ready soon."

I switch off the light to the entryway. Shoes lined every inch of the baseboard down the hallway, not even half of them my own, all untouched and unneeded. Let them house spiders and mice. I remain barefoot. I retrace my steps and veer left into my pallid kitchen, hand already on the lightswitch. Peeling linoleum, countertops hidden under piles of cans and boxes, but, I knew, battered. Covered with knife scars before I'd been forced to buy a cutting board. I peel my lips open. The cutting board was in the hosting room, covered in sausages cut to look like hearts, speared with bamboo picks. I check my watch. 2:34 am.

"I'll be ready soon." I flick the light off.

The living room is a single step away, lit only with lamps. Where the table used to be- my mattress, thrown down crooked. Two pillows, no blankets, one sheet. My laptop tossed carelessly on top, closed, the power cord slithering across the floor, under the couch, into the powerstrip in the only outlet in the room. I have to move the couch to get to it, cramming myself into the space behind. I speak through gritted teeth.

"I'll be ready soon." I unplug the three pronged cord and let it drop, losing it in the darkness. I push myself back upright. I don't bother moving the couch back.

I stumble onto my mattress as I cross the living room to the bathroom. The door ajar. The curtain rod is bare, the shelves empty. I turn to the mirror and stare at my face. My eyes fall down to scattered makeup around the sink. I pick up a lipstick and try pressing it to my lips- it catches and cakes. The color doesn't suit me at all. I wipe it off hurriedly with the back of my hand, and my eyes catch on my watch.

3:03 am.

I'm done with wandering from room to room for days on end, wearing down a path into the hardwood.

"I'll be ready soon."

The light in the room across from mine has been on since the beginning of all this.

I haven't once touched that door handle, despite seeing that light spill out from underneath the door every time I passed it. I left it and hoped it would burn out. It never did. I would never be ready to turn off this particular light.

I grit my teeth and quickly slam down the door handle, reaching blindly into the room, pressing my face into the wall as I search for the switch. Cobwebs coat my arm and burn fear into my skin that nearly makes my arm retreat into the safety of the darkness in the hallway—but I can feel it, there, the slick plate of the switch. I slam my hand into it and the light goes out.

I wrench my arm free and close the door, clinging onto the handle with both hands with all my strength, holding it closed, urgently muttering through my clenched teeth.

"I'm sorry. I'm sorry. I'm sorry. I'm sorry. I'll be ready soon."

I turn my back to the door and step back into the hosting room, the darkness crawling at my back. Once comfortable, now cloying. I walk to the table and pull the stationary from the centerpiece, resting it on the seat of one of the chairs, kneeling down, uncapping the pen, hesitating.

The lone light of the candle flickers. The food glistens.

I brush at my second-favorite dress.

I shake my matchbox.

I check my watch. 4:43 am.

I run out of things to check.

I set the pen on the paper.

YOU ARE INVITED!
A GATHERING HOSTED BY THE LAST PERSON
WILL TAKE PLACE FROM

I CHECK my watch. 4:43 am.

4:43 AM UNTIL THERE IS AN OUTSIDE AGAIN.
BRING YOUR FRIENDS!

I set the invitation back on the pedestal. "I'm ready. Come on in." Before I can think, I blow out the candle.

The contained darkness in my house presses in, and I quickly back up until my back hits the doorframe—I gasp for air and grab onto it so I can turn away from the table, facing the door across from what used to be mine. I rattle my matches, this time, unintentionally.

I open the box. I strike the first match. It lights up. I almost sigh in relief, but my vision finally focuses beyond the light, my golden hands, to two wet reflections in the dark. I blink, they don't. I open my mouth in a parody of a smile—and there's a fleshy noise as my first guest mimics the gesture.

My voice comes out thin. "I'm so glad to see you. Thank you for coming." I let the match burn down to my skin. It grows tight and hard with the heat until I'm forced to drop the seizing curled stick to the floor.

I strike the second match, it lights up. I'm already smiling, prepared this time. Dimly lit in front of me are two gnarled hands, resting at my second guest's sides—at my eye level. My smile almost falters as I look up, pinpricks of golden light dance off the teeth of something bent nearly double in the hallway to fit. Something warm and wet drips onto my cheek. "I'm so glad to see you. Thank you for coming." My skin blisters as the flame licks my fingers. I drop the match.

I chase the last match with my ruined fingers, clumsy. Striking the last match is agony. It nearly slips from my fingers even as I try to grip it. I press it to the box and quickly strike it. The match breaks in half, unlit.

The sound of the match head hitting the floor is drowned out by the sound of the door across from me opening, calmly. The sound overtakes all of my senses. Even in the dark, I close my eyes.

The uninvited guest steps out of the room, shoes clicking on the hardwood. In three steps, she's near me—I can hear her twirl. I can hear her lips peel open as she leans in from behind me. I know I'm supposed to run and turn the nearest light on. The nearest light is in her room. I can't.

She whispers. "Well?"

"I'm so glad to..." My words fade to nothing.

She waits. I clear my throat.

"Now we're all here."

The uninvited guest murmurs a "*Thank you*." She clicks into the hosting room. Three guests. Four mint colored plates. I open my eyes. I check my watch, as if it matters. Too dark. With shaking hands, I unbuckle it from my wrist, and drop it to the floor. I turn towards the hosting room. I walk to my seat, and try desperately to remember why I wanted this. My box of matches is clutched tightly in my hand. I shake it. I know it's empty. No matches left.

I take my seat. ◆

TWO STARS, WOULD NOT
RECOMMEND_
VELES SVITLYCHNY

Prudence | 1 Week Ago

Disappointing. This was the worst doppelganger game I've played yet! The occult twin had a terrible smell, like bitter cabbage, and it looked nothing like me! I had to make some substitutions, but I think we can all agree that they shouldn't have any effect on the end result.

I followed all of the steps, bundling nail clippings and hair together in a cloth and dabbing drops of blood on it. Then I buried it by an old tree in town. I knew that was a good place to bury it because all the locals avoid it. They murmured it was cursed whenever I deigned to listen in to their conversations (which was not often. I have better things to do with my time!)

Mother doesn't let me use sharp implements, even though I'm an adult. She says to me "you look like you'll cut your own fingers off" whenever I use a butter knife, and she absolutely forbade anything sharper than that. So, I waited until mother took her evening medicines and fell into her typical slumber to borrow the knife from the kitchen, along with a kitchen towel. The towel had old pink and brown stains like arabesques curlicuing across the threadbare surface. No one would miss this, I reckoned.

This knife was SHARP. I love holding it. I felt powerful, like I was truly free. Typically, mother clipped my nails for me (that characteristic *distrust*) and deposited them in her ash tray. I crept into her room and stood over her sleeping form as I felt around the nightstand. I wasn't worried. Nothing could wake her in this state. I found the ash tray, filled with those slender little crescents, so I sifted through the ash and half-smoked cigarillos until I found enough. I could have used fresh nails, but I abhor asymmetry, and the game called for *exactly* seven clippings.

Long story short, I plucked seven hairs from my scalp and bundled them along with the clippings in the kitchen towel. Pulling the knife across my thumb, it didn't even hurt. The blade just bit into my skin and opened up a lovely little gash. After dabbing the towel seven times, I sucked on my thumb until the bleeding stopped.

A warm summer wind blew across the field as I knelt before that old oak tree. They says that people got hung from that branch. I reckoned that was nonsense, but still, the branches were bare and strong. No leaves stirred. No one saw me but for the tree as I slouched away into that unanimous night.

Back home, I replaced the knife, being sure to wash it, of course! Mother mustn't know.

Mother didn't find the cut on my thumb until the seventh day. By then, the game was almost done, so after some prodding and punishments (which I deserved), I confessed what I did. She locked herself in her room and refused to talk to me. I didn't eat that night. Setting up my cot, I stretched out in the living room and counted the specks of mold on the ceiling: my usual ritual before sleep. There were fewer this time, and I couldn't reckon whether I slept that night. All I could think about was the emptiness inside. I smelled the creature before I saw it. Rotten cabbage! It came from Mother's room. The instructions said the twin could appear anywhere, so this seemed right. I knew I wasn't to interact with it, but I went into the kitchen and grabbed the knife just in case.

There was an apparition hunched over mother, limbs wilting and dripping to the ground. I screamed and, feeling free, plunged my knife through it. My eyes shut tight. Cold slime enveloped my hands up to the wrist, and then a bloom of warmth. Next thing I knew, the sun shone through the kitchen window. Scalding water, russet swirling down the drain. I never even learned anything from my twin. Mother didn't leave her room, and the smell is so much worse now. ◆

ABOUT THE AUTHORS_

RHIANNON RASMUSSEN is a nonbinary lesbian who lies on stacks of paper dreaming about teeth. For more writing & art, visit RHIANNONRS.COM. For shitposts & conversation, visit @CHARIBDYS on Twitter.

M.B. HARE is a writer and localizer based in the midwest. Their work's been published in *Ashes and Entropy*, *Vastarien*, *Cicada*, and other fine venues. Soon— terribly soon—they will publish a novel. It cannot be stopped. We've tried for so long, and it can't be stopped. Follow them at @MATTHEWBHARE

CASEY LUCAS is a writer, editor, and game developer who haunts the rocky shores of Aotearoa New Zealand. She is a two-time recipient of the Sir Julius Vogel Award for Best Short Story, New Zealand's highest honour in short form fantasy and science fiction. Apart from her short fiction, she is known for her fantasy horror web serial Into the Mire and her work on award-winning video games Mini Metro and Mini Motorways. She's @CASEYLUCAS on Twitter.

M. LYN HALL is a writer and illustrator from the southeast US, and @HARGRAF on Twitter. They are content to write about rituals and wagers gone horribly wrong, having given up on doing them ... for now.

SHI BRIGGS is an illustrator, graphic designer, and owner of Gross and Colorful- a weird and vibrant art shop. Their existence is long periods of dense fog dotted with furious bouts of stapling zines and cutting out stickers. They get too excited about stamps and monsters. @GROSSANDCOLORFUL on Instagram and TikTok.

VELES SVITLYCHNY is an author, dream weaver, visionary—plus podcaster. Formed from the iridescent chemical effluvia of the Raritan in New Jersey, they now live as a cryptid in the Pacific Northwest. They play many roles in the podcast No Rangers Allowed. When not pretending to be other people, they can be found on Twitter as @MEMORIOUSTULPA

ANDREY GARIN is a 24-year-old comic book artist and illustrator from Russia, Tyumen. Most of all he likes to work with science fiction, fantasy, or just something 'strange.' @STEGOCEPHAL on Twitter.

CPSIA information can be obtained
at www.ICGtesting.com
Printed in the USA
BVHW050436011221
622865BV00023B/1207